To my sweet children, Oskar and Amelie, who don't like it when I call them Ozzie and Amie. And to my wonderful husband, Brendan, whose name is not Brandon — A.D.

For Aisling and Beta — M.F.

Text © 2011 Annika Dunklee
Illustrations © 2011 Matthew Forsythe

Kids Can Press acknowledges the financial support of the Government of Ontario, through the Ontario Media Development Corporation's Ontario Book Initiative; the Ontario Arts Council; the Canada Council for the Arts; and the Government of Canada, through the BPIDP, for our publishing activity.

Published in Canada by
Kids Can Press Ltd.
25 Dockside Drive
Toronto, ON M5A 0B5

Published in the U.S. by
Kids Can Press Ltd.
2250 Military Road
Tonawanda, NY 14150

www.kidscanpress.com

The artwork in this book was rendered in pen and ink, gouache and digitally.
The text is set in Imagier.

Edited by Yvette Ghione
Designed by Marie Bartholomew

This book is smyth sewn casebound.
Manufactured in Shen Zhen, Guang Dong, P.R. China, in 3/2011 by Printplus Limited

CM 11 0 9 8 7 6 5 4 3 2 1

Library and Archives Canada Cataloguing in Publication

Dunklee, Annika, 1965–
        My name is Elizabeth! / written by Annika Dunklee ; illustrated by Matthew Forsythe.
ISBN 978-1-55453-560-6

I. Forsythe, Matthew, 1976– II. Title.

PS8607.U542M96 2011   jC813'.6   C2011-900088-1

Kids Can Press is a Corus™ Entertainment company

My Name Is Elizabeth!

Written by Annika Dunklee

Illustrated by Matthew Forsythe

Kids Can Press

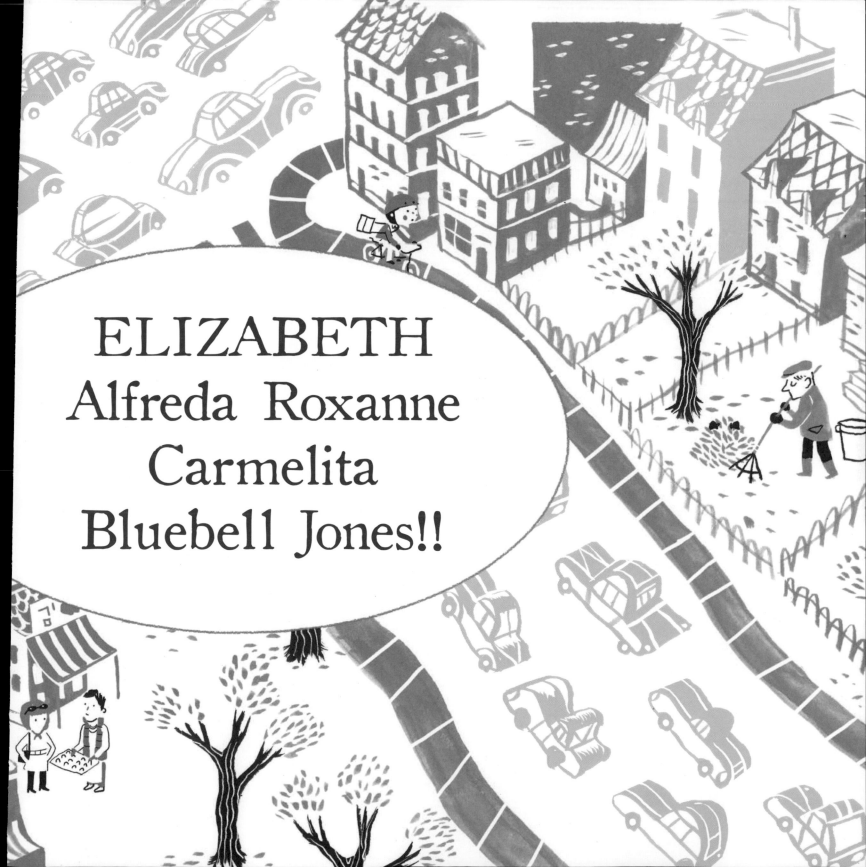